This book belongs to:

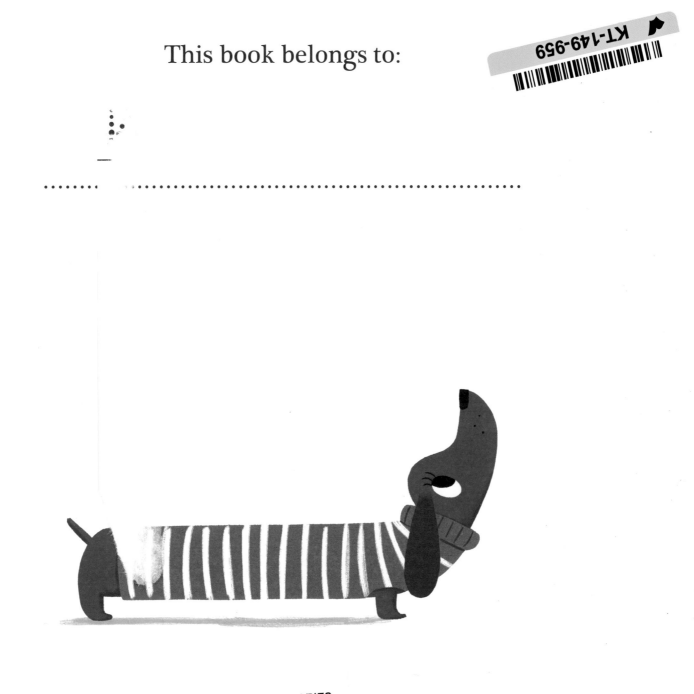

For Emily and Robin M.B.
For Leo N.S.

First published in 2014 by
Hodder Children's Books
This edition published in 2015

Text copyright © Mara Bergman 2014
Illustration copyright © Nicola Slater 2014

Hodder Children's Books
338 Euston Road, London NW1 3BH

Hodder Children's Books Australia
Level 17/207 Kent Street, Sydney, NSW 2000

The right of Mara Bergman to be identified
as the author and Nicola Slater as the
illustrator of this Work has been asserted
by them in accordance with the Copyright,
Designs and Patents Act 1988.

A catalogue record of this book is available
from the British Library.

ISBN: 978 1 444 91420 7
10 9 8 7 6 5 4 3 2 1

Printed in China

Hodder Children's Books is a
division of Hachette Children's Books.
An Hachette UK Company

www.hachette.co.uk

Best Friends

Mara Bergman   Nicola Slater

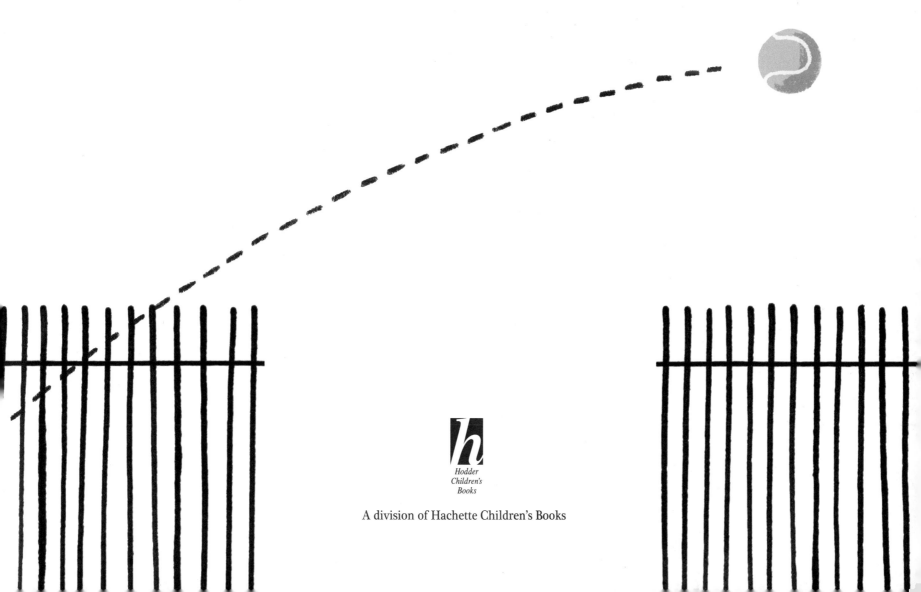

Hodder
Children's
Books

A division of Hachette Children's Books

Dexter McFadden McSimmons McClean,
the dog with the longest legs anyone's seen,
was chasing a ball as fast as he could,
over the bridge and into the wood.

Meanwhile...

Daisy the dachshund
was strolling along,
humming and whistling
to her favourite song.

She ignored the dark

FLASH

as it shot through the wood

and followed her ball just as fast as she could.

Meanwhile...

Lily had been for a wash and a cut
when she went to the park for a walk and a strut.

She too was chasing
her favourite ball,
ignoring the other dogs,
big ones and small.

Three dogs
were running.
Where would
they go?

and **Daisy**
SO slow,

Dexter like lightning

and **Lily**, who hated to dirty her claws,

ran ever so lightly
on tippy-toe paws.

Meanwhile...

William was running
as fast as he could,
calling for Dexter,
who ran through
the wood,

while…

Jack was happily
strolling along,
looking for Daisy
and singing a song,

and…

Maddie was searching
and searching for Lily,
who'd just had her hair cut
and looked rather silly!

"Dexter!"
called William,

then Jack,
"Daisy, here!"

Maddie
called, "Lily!"

But did they appear?

The Millers were having a picnic that day

and **jumped up** as Dexter came charging their way,

and Daisy gave someone
a terrible
fright...

while Lily got mixed up
with somebody's kite.

Sandwiches, newspapers, blankets went flying,

and one little baby kept
crying and **crying!**

But soon they were off again,
dashing about, ignoring each call,
every cry, every shout.

"*Dexter!*" called William,

then Jack, "*Daisy, here!*"

Maddie called, "*Lily!*"

But did they appear?

THEN...

the children grew worried. What was that sound?
They ran to the stream...

SPLISH!

SPLASH!

...and look what they found:

Dexter and Daisy
and Lily all wet!

Each was the soggiest, happiest pet.
With a **wriggle** and **shake,** the dogs made a splatter.
The children got soaked, but it didn't matter!

And this is the way that our story ends –
the children and dogs became…

best friends!

Look out for these other great picture books,
perfect to share with children:

SNIP SNAP, ALLIGATOR!
Mara Bergman and Nick Maland

SNIP SNAP, LOOK WHO'S BACK!
Mara Bergman and Nick Maland

Six Dinner Sid
INGA MOORE

OI FROG!
KES GRAY & JIM FIELD

WANTED: The Perfect Pet
'A hoot.' THE SUNDAY TIMES
Fiona Roberton